To the mother of the child and all the believers
—M. T.D.

To my mother, who put the magic in my childhood
—E. S. V.

The Star of Christmas
Text copyright © 2009 by Maria T. DiVencenzo
Illustrations copyright © 2009 by Elaine Verstraete
All rights reserved.
Library of Congress Cataloging-in-Publication Data
DiVencenzo, Maria T. The Star of Christmas / by Maria T. DiVencenzo;
illustrated by Elaine Verstraete.-1st ed. p. cm. Summary: One Christmas
Eve, a child is asked by the ornaments on her Christmas tree to answer the
question: Who is the "Star" of Christmas? ISBN 978-0-9816003-0-7
[1. Christmas—Fiction. 2. Christmas trees—Fiction. 3. Christmas tree
ornaments—Juvenile Fiction.] I. Verstraete, Elaine, ill. II. Title.
Library of Congress Control Number: 2008924007
The text type is Granjon. The illustrations are watercolor.
Designer: Amy Manzo Toth. Editor: Rebecca Davis. Printed in U.S.A.
Published by Winterlake Press, a division of Winterlake Communications, Inc.,
P.O. Box 1274, Buffalo, NY 14231-1274. www.winterlakepress.com
First Edition 10 9 8 7 6 5 4 3 2 1

Thank you to Chloe for her charming
smile and delightful manner.

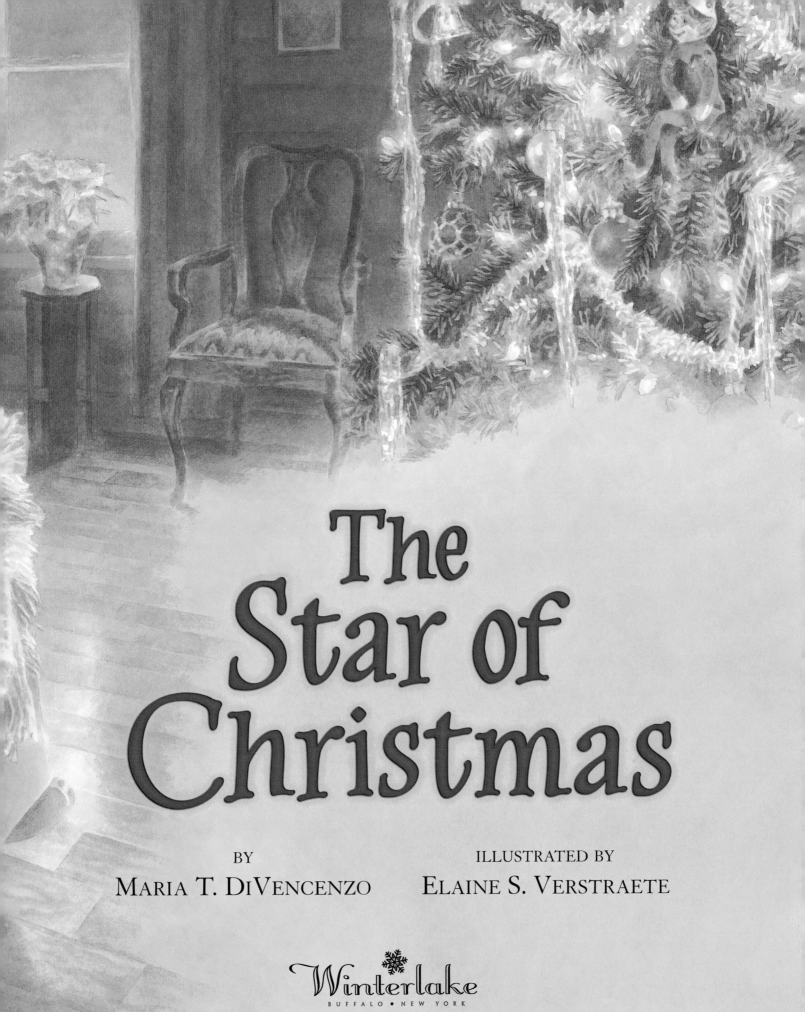

The Star of Christmas

BY
MARIA T. DIVENCENZO

ILLUSTRATED BY
ELAINE S. VERSTRAETE

Winterlake
BUFFALO • NEW YORK

Snuggled in my chair near the Christmas tree, I took a deep breath of the pine, peppermint, sugar-cookie sweetness that filled the living room. The great-grandpa clock ticktocked behind me and I clucked along, trying to stay awake. But my eyelids drooped with each tick, and I pulled my blanket close, my clucks soon becoming yawns.

"I know what we should do!" A bright voice suddenly rang out. "Let's ask the child."

Swallowing a yawn, I sat straight up. Was the Christmas tree talking?

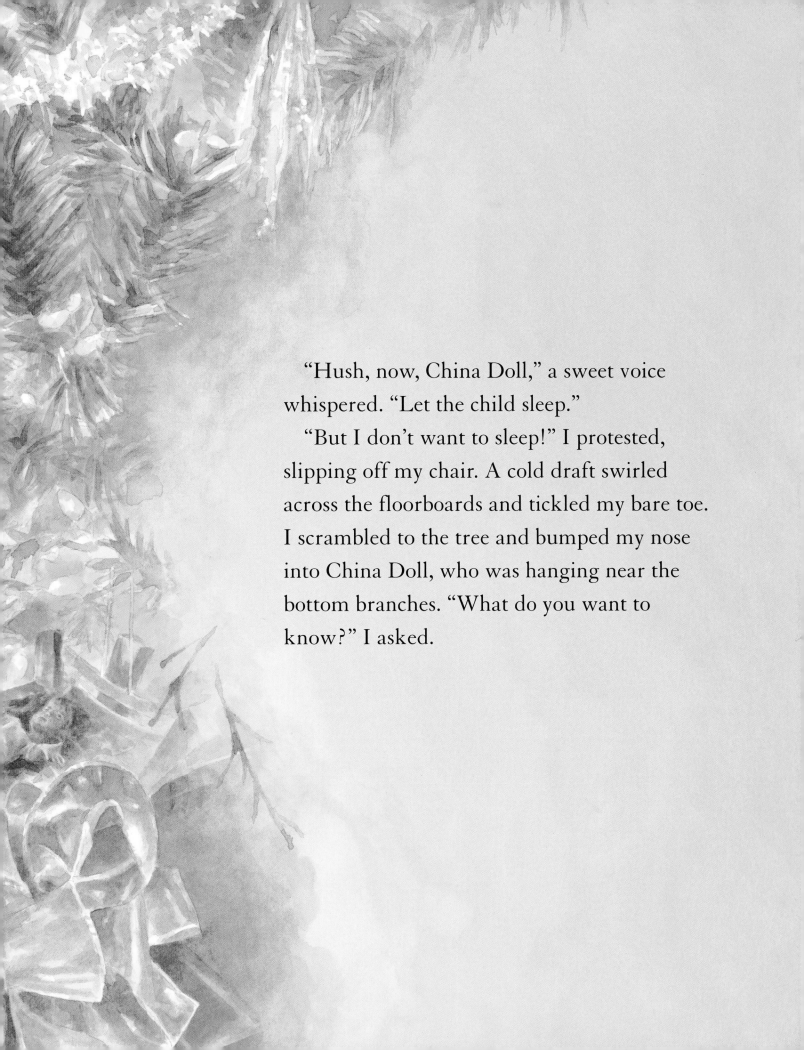

"Hush, now, China Doll," a sweet voice whispered. "Let the child sleep."

"But I don't want to sleep!" I protested, slipping off my chair. A cold draft swirled across the floorboards and tickled my bare toe. I scrambled to the tree and bumped my nose into China Doll, who was hanging near the bottom branches. "What do you want to know?" I asked.

China Doll slid down a strand of silver garland, then waltzed around my feet in a whirl of brown curls and red velvet. "Who is the star of Christmas, child?" she asked.

"The star of Christmas?" I said. "What do you mean?"

China Doll stopped waltzing. She smoothed her skirt and raised one perfect brow. "Don't you know? The star of Christmas is Christmas's V-I-P: very important person," she explained. "You might even call it the V-*M*-I-P of Christmas: very *most* important part! Do you know who it is?"

"Why, of course I do!" I quickly answered.

"Then tell them!" China Doll waved at the branches on the tree. "Tell all the other ornaments that I am the star of Christmas. Night after night we bicker, bicker, bicker about it. Someone must settle our disagreement, and I pick you!"

"But why do you think that you're the star of Christmas?" I asked.

"Because Christmas is beautiful! It's full of sparkle and shine, just like I am. Why, it only makes sense that I am the star of Christmas."

"Christmas is beautiful, China Doll," I said, scooping her up and hugging her close. "You are beautiful, too. But you're not the star of Christmas. The star of Christmas is—"

"Ta-da! It's good old Gift Box!"
Holding China Doll tightly, I spun around. Not far
above the tree's red skirt, I spotted the ornament that
looked exactly like a shiny present.

"So you think that you're the star of Christmas?"
I asked, pulling Gift Box off the tree.

"Well, of course, I am," he said, puffing curly ribbons out of his eyes. "I'm nice to look at *and* I have a surprise inside. What would Christmas be without me? Ta-da! Surprise! It's good old Gift Box! The star of Christmas!"

"Oh, I love Christmas surprises!" I cried. Holding his little box belly close to my ear, I shook the present this way and that. "I wish I could see what's hiding inside you, Gift Box! But you're not the star of Christmas. The star of Christmas is—"

"Yoo-hoo! Little person?" A shriek and a squeak interrupted me. "Oh, yoo-hoo!"

A tiny man wearing jingle-bell slippers was standing on a clump of branches in the middle of the tree, swaying to and fro like a surfer balancing on a furry green sea.

"Jolly Old Elf, you're going to fall!" I cried, jumping up to catch him. But I was too late. The elf flipped off his perch, somersaulted down the tree, and landed with a *thump* on my cold toe.

"I bet you're trying to tell me that you're the star of Christmas, little man," I said, lifting him by the jingle-bell tip of his hat.

"Yes, I am!" The pixie knocked three times on the side of Gift Box and asked, "Did you figure out what's inside this present? Is it a rag doll I sewed? A puzzle I puzzled over?"

"You know the rules, Jolly Old Elf," I scolded. "No peeking till Christmas. It's a surprise!"

"I know it's a surprise! I make Christmas surprises and give Christmas its magic!" Jolly Old Elf began to kick one spindly leg after the other, wriggling and twirling and tinkling his jingle bells. Then he winked at me. "Christmas is magic, child. I am magic! No surprise about it, I'm your star of Christmas."

"Christmas is magic, Jolly Old Elf," I said. "But you're not the star of Christmas. The star of Christmas is—"

"Fa-la-la-la-la-la-la-la-la!"

A bell chimed and I hurried to the middle of the tree, where I knew I'd find Silver Bell. Reaching into the soft branches, I tapped her little body till it began to sway back and forth.

"Let me guess! Christmas is music, right, Silver Bell?"

Silver Bell rocked hard and fast, until her singing and ringing drowned even the ticking of the clock. "My carols make Christmas merry, so I must be the star of Christmas. Sing with me now, everybody! Stop all this silliness and sing!"

I couldn't help it. I set China Doll, Gift Box, and Jolly Old Elf down, and we marched around the Christmas tree belting out a chorus of rum-pum-pums. "Oh, Silver Bell," I finally exclaimed above her dings and dongs. "You are merry and bright. But you're not the star of Christmas. The star of Christmas is—"

"Me, me, me! Don't forget about me, me, *me*!"

"Teddy Bear, how could I ever forget you?" I said, standing on tiptoe and poking her round belly. She giggled, then fell into my arms, squeezing me tight. "You're just like my lovey, except you have two button eyes instead of one, and lots more fur and stuffing."

"That's me, me, me! Your loved one. Your best furry friend!" Teddy Bear said. "Christmas is for loved ones and friends. Think of holiday cards, Christmas cookies, parties, and feasts! They are all for family friends, furry friends, new friends and old. That makes me, me, *me* the star of Christmas!"

"Christmas is about family and friends, Teddy Bear," I said. "But you're not the star of Christmas. The star of Christmas is—"

"I've said it a thousand times," a thick, old voice crackled, "for hundreds of years!"

I looked up at Wise King, who was seated on a throne above my head, his white beard spilling down his velvet robe like a frozen waterfall.

"Do you think you're the star of Christmas, Wise King?" I asked, trying to curtsy in spite of my sleeper pajamas.

"Christmas is about giving," Wise King said. "Correct?"

"Yes, Your Majesty!" I said.

"And I gave the first Christmas present, demonstrating charity to all. Correct?"

"Yes, Your Majesty!" I shouted.

"Well, then, it seems reasonable to conclude that I am the star of Christmas."

"Actually, the star of Christmas is . . ." I paused for a moment, wondering what such a king might do to someone in his kingdom who dared to correct him.

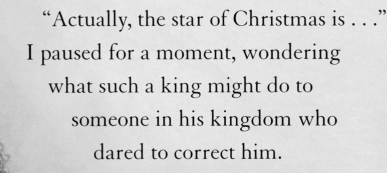

"She means to say, Your Highness, that you're not the star of Christmas," a snow-white bird cooed.
Startled, I stepped back.
Gentle Dove flew from her nest and hovered over me. The clock ticktocked loudly in my ears as I tried to listen to her soft voice.

"Christmas is charity, Wise King. But even more, Christmas is peace." Gentle Dove landed softly on the two fingers I held out for her. "Peace stirs the kindness and compassion in each of us. Every Christmas, I soar far and wide, settling all corners of the world with peace. That is why I am the star of Christmas."

"Hush, everyone." The sweet voice was whispering again. "Let the child speak!"

Climbing onto a chair, I reached up to the very tip-top of the tree for Crystal Angel, whose golden halo shone above all the branches, tinsel, and lights.

"You know!" I exclaimed, lifting her gently from her bough. "You know who the star of Christmas is, don't you, Crystal Angel?"

Crystal Angel smiled at me. "Tell them, child," she whispered.

The clock ticktocked. Silent, waiting, the ornaments stared up at me from the tree's red skirt. I wiggled my cold, bare toe and looked back at their wondering faces.

"You are very special ornaments," I said, "important parts of Christmas, each and every one."

"Tell us, child!" China Doll called out.

"Do tell, child!" Jolly Old Elf exclaimed. "Who is the star of Christmas?"

"I will tell you," I answered. "But first I'll show you."

I knelt down by the red skirt and cradled
the ornament that was hanging on the bare,
broken branches at the bottom of the tree.
"It's the *child*," I whispered.

Together we watched the simple wooden
manger rock through the silent night.